Dying Hour

Jennifer Rouse Barbeau

Books by Jennifer Rouse Barbeau

Fiction:
Swampy Jo (Your Scrivener Press)

Dying Hour

Jennifer Rouse Barbeau

For information about permission to reprint, record, or perform
sections of this book, write **Fluid Grouse Press**, 635 Scollard Street,
North Bay, Ontario, Canada P1B 5A2

Library and Archives Canada Cataloguing in Publication

Rouse Barbeau, Jennifer, 1963-, author

Dying Hour / Jennifer Rouse Barbeau

Cover Design: Jennifer Rouse Barbeau
Cover Photo: Photo by Jason Rosewell on Unsplash
Author Photo: Nicolas Barbeau

ISBN: 978-1-7751389-4-5

This novel is dedicated to my husband, Barry Grills.

CONTENTS

ACKNOWLEDGMENTS

Thanks to Maggie Lacroix of Wynterblue Publishing Canada Inc., who is a fearless spirit and the organizer of the WynLit 73-hour Novel Marathon of 2009, during which I wrote the first draft of this novella.

'Dying Hour' is a hybrid novella: part prose, part audio play, part stage play, and can be read in any of these guises.

CHARACTERS

STAGE CHARACTERS
Central Character:
- STAN TEMPLEMAN, an overweight man, 32, with a booming voice, who works as a late night radio talk show host

Secondary Characters:
- PETER BAINSBRIDGE, acoustic rock star
- STAN'S DAD, Frank, at the ages of 35 and 45
- STAN'S MAMA, Gail, at the ages of 30, 40 and 50

VOICE CHARACTERS
- TIMOTHY, a nine year old boy, calling on his mom's cell phone
- A VARIETY OF ADULT CALLERS, MALE AND FEMALE

TIME
The present, November, over several nights from midnight to six in the morning.
Presented in 2 Acts.

PLACE
A radio sound-booth/studio in a small city.

Stage Setting:

A mid-tone brown backdrop wall has a simple interior door on its left which leads to a stark white hallway; a large white-and-black Westclox clock hangs on the interior wall, toward the right. Centre stage is nearly filled with a dining-room-table-sized work station, with computer equipment to one side, and two ceiling-mounted microphones above. Two chairs on casters tuck into the table, near the wall.

An imaginary wall of reflective glass separates this sound studio from the audience, whose members watch the action from a position that would be inside the unused sound engineer's booth.

ACT I, Scene 1
Open for Worship

Stan Templeman's big frame fills the stingy doorway, black silhouette against a sharp white rectangle of light. He holds the sound studio's simple, flat door fully open for a moment, perusing the dark interior appreciatively. Beyond this doorway is a white hall through which Stan has just come. He squints a bit in the light from the hall, but his eyes relax as he moves into the darkened studio space.

STAN: "I'm home," *he says, launching a booming laugh.*

Stan, it's obvious, is a big man, all around. Big body. Big heart. Big voice.

Stan hums to himself and smiles as he gives

a hip check to a heavy bag hanging on his arm, urging it through the doorway. Stan clicks the door shut in a practiced back-kick. The door disappears from view into a long expanse of wall that is painted the colour of strong coffee with a shot of Bailey's. The studio is in all but total darkness. He flicks on a computer monitor in the dark; the machine makes an audible click. The screen shines up at him, spreading light and shooting shadows from his chin and nose up along the rounded terrain of his face.

Stan swings the bag off his shoulder and onto the floor, to nestle in the semi-darkness at the foot of his wheeled desk chair, like a favourite pet. A plastic-wrapped hero sandwich spills out from the bag, onto the floor. Stan sweeps down with one beefy arm to scoop it up, while he slips the other arm out of the sleeve of his coat. He juggles the sandwich from one hand to the other to complete the removal of the garment, and shakes the short wool jacket to clear a fine dusting of snow from the lapel, while he places the sandwich beside his computer. He folds the coat over the chair back, humming all the while.

Stan is a happy man.

Stan's computer and screen are one small part of a small city of black-boxed digital technology anchored to a circular expanse of table that fills the centre of this studio room. Stan reaches down and empties the contents of his shoulder bag onto the table top: chocolate bars, pop, chips, and the like.

STAN: "Just like Mama's kitchen," *he says, admiring the spread.*

Stan now takes the folded coat and hangs it over the back of his desk chair, brushing the jacket's shoulder line as if the chair back were Stan's much-loved child. From behind the chair, he adjusts a bright red Remembrance Day poppy on the jacket's lapel, making sure it is well secured. He pats the coat heartily on one arm, and turns to check the time on the large Westclox on the wall behind him. The clock ticks, and one long black arm on the white face moves a single second closer to midnight.

Stan stands up straight. He walks around the large round pedestal table, and leans his back against it a moment. Then he pats his ample belly, and turns sideways to admire his full girth in the dim reflection on the half wall of glass that faces his work station. Beyond the glass reflection is the sound engineer's booth, as empty and hollow as a grave. It is from this dead space, where time and man do not exist, that we, Stan's audience, watch.

Stan pulls at his belly for a moment, lifting it closer to his chest to hold a pose. Mama appears off to his left.

MAMA: "Like a truckdriver, my son Stan. And his voice? Waah!"

The flesh on her upper arms flaps with the down-stroke of her two fat little hands.

MAMA: "At two years old he sounded like

a man who'd smoked a pack a day for a lifetime! What could my little Stan Templeman do but go into radio?"

Stan faces his glass reflection again.

STAN: "Mama's happy boy," *he says.*

His smile freezes, then droops. He reaches into his back pocket and pulls out a small silver flask, marked with age but gleaming. What little light there is in the studio bounces off its metal curves, and Stan smiles at it. He puts the flask to his mouth and takes a quick swallow before placing it in his breast pocket.

Stan turns back to the low stack of computer boxes, making switch selections with ease. A small festival of coloured lights sparkles on his face as he takes his station.

STAN: "The countdown to party is on . . ."

Stan's voice is all bass. It seems to boom through the studio, shaking the glass partition that once held a sound technician; the invisible wall that separates Stan from the past. For a dozen years now, Stan has used that voice to earn his coin. His voice started out old, and never grew younger. It never grew older, either, but it did grow wider. By the time Stan was sixteen, his voice squatted around him like hovercraft padding when he spoke. People moved away from it, even as they smiled at Stan. His voice is the rumbly kind that stays low to the ground, picking up dirt and gravel as it strokes the earth, and then rises to belly level to sock you in the gut. Stan, when he speaks, is a mountain. And once he began to smoke, late in his teens, his voice trolled even lower to the ground, picking up blacker gravel than it had when he was young.

Stan checks the Westclox. The two black needle hands meet at the top, in silent prayer. Stan commands a digital music cue with a poke from one square fingertip, and a flourish of sultry cello notes, underscored by piano, escapes. He brings one cup of a pair of headphones near one ear, and all but kisses the mike with his mouth.

STAN: "Good eventide, all you lost souls and sad sisters in our lusty, rusty city tonight."

The darkness around Stan seems to snuggle in closer.

STAN: "Stan your Temple Man is here to soothe your sorrows with a little . . . r and b."

He enunciates clearly, the 'd' in 'and' pinching at the air. Another flicked switch and a sax takes over. Stan sits back. After a moment, he flicks another switch and the studio is quiet, the way Stan likes it. The small window of screen that holds his songs and programs, his sound effects and cues, and all his bits of wisdom, shines up at Stan as if he were the fountain of all knowledge. He eyes the long facing wall of glass as if it held a mural.

A red light blinks: Stan's cue.

STAN: "Oh yesss, my flock of late night listeners, the Temple is open. Stan Templeman here, body and soul."

The 'd' in 'and' stings the air again.

STAN: "It is a murky, murky November night for one and all. But as we all know, anything could happen now that Stan is in the building. Weather shifts in its patterns, the axis of the earth leans infinitesimally to the right or to the left, and you, my dear listeners, tell all. The lines are now open and the night is long, so please, please, tell me what's in your world tonight. Get your dialing fingers going to 1-800-YOU-TELL, to call me here at the station."

Another sax solo and a haunting non-melody in a woman's voice.

The phones stay silent.

STAN: "Lines one, two, three and four are open, my friends, waiting for your words. Each phone line has its own distinctive ring, so that Stan the Temple Man can tell you all apart."

A laugh, rich and deep.

STAN: "While we wait to decide what ails our sleeping city this cold November night, Stan will paint a picture of what I see inside these studio walls. I have a magic window here. A broad, unclaimed territory of windows that enclose the space where our station's sound technician used to be. All that's behind us now— as gone as ghosts—with digital software and hardware doing the job of one man in less gigabytes than it takes to download a Christina Aguilara video. So it's quiet here, in studio one. Quiet as a church."

Stan almost whispers the word.

STAN: "So here I sit, with this massive black canvas of mirrors reflecting . . . well, anything I want it to reflect. The glass is black, from where I see it, and shines at the slightest hint of light. It looks to me like a night sky, much like the one that we call 'real' outside these studio walls. But my night sky is a summer sky. November does not exist here. My mirror of sky is soft and gentle. Smelling of summer: of fresh-mown grass and dirty feet. Of chlorine or seaweed, depending on your income level. My sky twinkles and winks at me, and would to you, too, if you were here."

Stan breathes in deeply, and exhales: a long, leisurely moan.

STAN: "I can almost hear the crickets."

Stan inserts the introductory rift for a bit of old summer rock.

STAN: "Crickets count out the degrees of warmth in a summer night, I'm told. The hotter the weather, the more they 'crick'. This is a scientific fact. Count a cricket's cricks per minute and multiply by ten, and you've got yourself an accurate temperature reading. In Farenheit, mind you. Do you remember Farenheit, in our days before Celsius became our weather measure of choice? The numbers were bigger, but hey, the sweat on your skin felt the same. Didn't it?"

And the summer tune fills in the blanks. The song fills the air, growing louder as the studio grows darker, until only the Westclox clock face can be seen, its white face as large as a summer moon. The hour hand moves. Suddenly it is . . .

TWO A.M. The sandwich on the table is gone, and in its place is a ball of plastic wrap, a chocolate bar wrapper, and a crushed pop can.

Stan laughs, teeters backward in his chair at a dangerous angle. One toe lingers on the underside ledge of the table. Stan fishes out the little metal flask from his breast pocket, and looks toward the far end of the bank of glass windows that cover the length of the sound studio. STAN'S DAD appears; he is facing away from Stan, looking at a newspaper in his hand. He takes a small silver flask from his breast pocket, identical to the flask that Stan holds at the sound desk. Stan lifts his flask toward his dad, in a salute, and both men down a quick swig before returning their respective flasks to a breast pocket. STAN'S DAD wanders off, reading the newspaper, and fades into the darkness.

Stan smiles at the spot where the apparition was. He winces, shakes his head, and laughs.

A call is in progress.

STAN: "So, Ted from Aberdeen Road, you called him a *what*?"

MALE CALLER: "I called him a soaker."

STAN: "A soaker. Like what happens to your feet when you step in a mud puddle, and all the muck and goo squishes into your shoes and through your socks, and between your toes. Uuuhh. That's such an awful feeling."

MALE CALLER: "Yup. He deserved it too. Soaker that he is."

Stan laughs heartily, and looks at the clock. The room grows dark. The round Westclox face grows luminous, and the hour hand moves to . . .

FOUR A.M.

Heavy metal rock pounds against the studio floor. Stan scoots along the edge of the circular centre table on his wheeled desk chair, playing air guitar, then pushes himself back into position with a single, short-legged thrust.

STAN: "So, fine listeners, we have made it through the Musak hours and into the humble, troubled, hectic span of the foursees, when trouble can be had, just for the asking. Haven't done the dirty deed yet? Heck, who's gonna catch you at this hour? Might as well go for it. The foursees. When sleeplessness moves through resignation toward productivity again. Not asleep yet? Hell, why keep trying. Might as well get up now. Am I right, fine listeners? AM I RIGHT?!"

Stan fishes through the debris on his desk. What he really wants is another drag on a cigarette, but there just isn't time before tonight's interview arrives.

STAN: "Yee-esss, ladies and lads, the night is long, and sometimes lonely."

Stan hisses at the mike which he now cups in one hand.

STAN: "But your ever-friend Stan, Stan the friendly Temple Man, is here with you, for you, filling out the lonely spaces with . . . well, with what? What do I offer you, the listener I never see, wandering out in the world while I sit alone in the dark? Companionship? The same lost and floundering spirit as you, alone at night, with nowhere to settle my thoughts?"

Stan lets go of the mike, and looks at it, like it was his father, who never made any sense to Stan.

STAN: "Yesssss, that is what I am. That is who I do. I am a companion in the dark. And here's another number for you, as we await the only other human creature fool enough to roam the empty night with you, and me, at this ungodly hour . . . the only man who would agree to be interviewed, live, at four in the morning, when the rest of the world is sleeping, buried in mounds of dreams and blankets, while you and I bay at the moon."

Stan can almost see the moon, reflected in the mirrors of the sound booth windows: a round and fuzzy shape, whiter than the rest of the shadows clinging to the glass.

STAN: "The moon and all its mystery, the moon which is still here with me, in my perpetual summer-night window: actually, that's my own smiling face I see, reflected in this little studio's glass partitions . . ."

Stan laughs.

STAN: " . . . a happy, man-in-the-moon face, shining down on our many yesterdays and our indefinite tomorrows, and only once on this single present day we all share."

Stan smiles at his own reflection.

STAN: "So let's set up this mystery man interview for you, with a sample of his own kind of magic. Sink into this, all you night owls out there. This man is a local sensation. A one man band. Plays a mean stick! He's made a name for himself on the Internet, and moved from the virtual world into the real one, to be with you in clubs around our fair city. Here he is, ladies and lads, lovers and losers . . . the one and only Peter Bainsbridge."

Stan passes the audience over to technology. A digital version of Peter Bainsbridge on acoustic guitar momentarily fills the air, but Stan presses it out of existence with a square fingertip. The man would be here in a moment, and Stan hates those entrances where creator and creation come together as if rehearsed.

STAN (to himself): "No orchestrated entrance, please. Let's not go for the American blockbuster moment, shall we? Can't bear that kind of falsehood, not in the middle of a clean, honest night. Like this one. Like all of them. But still and all, let us prepare for our guest."

Stan says this aloud, though his radio listeners can't hear him.

He folds his laptop lid shut. With the laptop screen hidden, the room plunges into shadow. The Westclox timepiece on the wall glows bright. The clock's second-hand clicks into place at . . .

FOUR TWENTY A.M.

Stan flicks on a light over his head, on the microphone's stem, and flips open his laptop.

STAN: "So, Pete. Buddy. So, you videotape yourself playing your songs on one of your five guitars in your father's basement."

PETER BAINSBRIDGE: "Yup."

STAN: "And then you edit the videos, using the edit software in your dad's handicam."

PETER BAINSBRIDGE: " 'A'sright."

STAN: "And then you upload those same, fine videos to the 'net."

PETER BAINSBRIDGE: "Uh huh."

STAN: "And that simple process has allowed you to make nearly a hundred thousand dollars this year alone in advertising partnerships and concert revenues."

PETER BAINSBRIDGE: "Yeah."

Stan pauses a moment. Taps his fingers on the table. The sound echoes through the studio like bongo drums.

STAN: "Well, Peter Bainsbridge, I have to

thank you on behalf of our many late night visitors for taking the time to come out here after your last set, to talk to us about how you became such an overnight success."

PETER BAINSBRIDGE: "Well, I worked hard for my success. You know, I took guitar lessons for eight years, and then practiced, like, all the time."

Stan nods. Peter nods. Stan's fingers tap again.

PETER   BAINSBRIDGE: "Practice, practice, practice."

STAN: "Wise words, Peter. Well, again, thank you Peter for sharing your plan with Stan the Temple Man and our listeners. It's been . . . revealing. Very revealing. And I wish you all the success possible with this venture."

PETER BAINSBRIDGE: "Thanks, Stan. It's an honour to come to the Temple and tell my story."

Stan smiles.

STAN: "The honour is mine, Peter. It is. Now here, ladies and lads, is another cut from Peter's newest album, 'Alone in Time'. Available through   local   retailers   and   online   at peterbainsbridgealonedotcom."

The song crests, and fades.

Stan leans forward, elbows on his thighs, and hangs his head.

Peter stretches in his chair.

PETER BAINSBRIDGE: "That was fun."

Stan nods, head still hanging near his knees.

STAN: "Yes. Yes, it was, Peter. But, man, I don't know if we can stretch this out for a week's worth of late night interviews, like I thought we might."

PETER BAINSBRIDGE: "Oh no?"

Stan rattles his head. Cleans the dirt from under a thumbnail.

STAN: "I don't think so, Pete. I mean, you've got a great story. A really great story. You've made it, man, and almost nobody gets that. But, I think we've said all there is to say on the subject."

Peter nods. Sits up. Cocks his head to one side, then nods again.

PETER BAINSBRIDGE: "Okay. So what'll you do, then, with the rest of the week?"

Stan sits up too. Claps Peter on the arm, and shakes his hand hard.

STAN: "No worries, Peter. No worries. We'll find some kind of excitement to fill the gaps. All the best, Peter. Thanks, again."

And he shuffles Peter out through the flat, un-panelled door. The moment Peter is gone, Stan collapses spread eagle on his desk chair and holds his head in his hands.

STAN: "Painful. Painful, painful."

The phone rings, startling Stan. He picks up the receiver.

STAN: "Yes. Mister Edwards. Ernie. Yes,

just finished. He's on his way. Yeah, I had to really work for it. Every word. Mmhmm. I thought so too. Well, you can't always predict these things. Yes, I do know that. I'm aware . . . yes, I know the station could close . . . No, I wouldn't want to see that either. I love this job . . . Mmhm . . . right. It's the isolation I like. I mean the, um, the . . . the *solitude*. Yeah. Being your own boss, and all that . . . Well no, not technically . . . Uh huh. Okay. I'm sure I'll think of something to get the callers in. Yes. We'll draw in those advertising dollars. Yes. I'll keep you posted. Alright then. Thanks for calling."

Stan replaces the receiver. He looks at the swell of the handset for a long time. He fishes the little vial from his pocket, and drains it.

The clockface on the wall seems to grow brightly, and the studio dims. Clock hands move to . . .

FIVE A.M.

STAN: "This is Stan, the Temple Man, coming to you from inside your radio in the Dying Hour of five ay em."

A phone rings. Stan jumps a little, and answers quickly.

WOMAN CALLER: "So why's it the dying hour? Are you, like, sick?"

STAN: "I am, in a way, m'lady. I am always, even after twelve years of this midnight to six shift, I am always sick unto death in the fifth hour of the wee morning. My chest gets tight and my stomach cramps and I feel like the very air I breathe is being squeezed from my lungs. Every five ay em. And it lasts about an hour. I am sure that I will die of a heart attack at five ay em some day in my future.

WOMAN CALLER: "Wow."

STAN: "What about you, m'lady? What do you think will happen to you? How do you predict that you will die, when your time comes?"

The woman caller pauses. Stan looks at the digital caller ID screen on his phone, and tries to focus.

WOMAN CALLER: "I think I'll die in a train accident."

STAN: "A train accident. Oh now, that's interesting. A big, catastrophic train accident? Or a little bitty, railcar-falling-over-with-a-bump kind of accident?"

WOMAN CALLER: "Big," *the woman says.* "Fire, maybe. And a whole pile up of derailed train cars."

Stan whistles.

STAN: "Any idea of when this might happen? Time of day? Season? Weather conditions?"

WOMAN CALLER: "Hmm. Maybe in the spring. Lots of mud and guck, stuck to the windows after. Blending with the blood of everyone."

STAN: "Will you see that when you're

dead?"

WOMAN CALLER: "No. Definitely not. I'll be very, very dead."

Stan hiccups on a laugh.

STAN: "So, do you take the train, much?"

WOMAN CALLER: "Never. Not ever."

STAN: "No wonder why."

He fills in with another song so he can eat a pepperoni stick. The pepperoni makes him feel a little better. He tries to take a swig from the empty flask to wash it down. The phone rings again.

STAN (wiping his mouth): "You've reached Stan, the Temple Man," *he says.* "In the Dying Hour."

TIMOTHY: "Hullo, mister Temple. I'm Timothy."

Stan, startled, struggles to swallow the last of the meat stick. The kid on the line can't be more than seven: his voice is high and weightless.

STAN: "I'm sorry, son, but you must have the wrong number. This . . . this is an adult radio show. It's . . ." *Stan bends toward the Westclox face.* " . . . after five in the morning. Is everything okay? Do you need anything?"

TIMOTHY: "I'm just up, is all. I heard you on my laptop. I thought maybe I'd call and tell you when I think I'll die."

Stan looks at the digital ID window on the phone. 'Unknown', it says.

STAN: "Where are you calling from, son? What did you say your name was, again?"

TIMOTHY: "It's Timothy."

STAN: "Timothy. Okay, Timothy, um, where are you calling from? Are you sure you're okay?"

Stan can hear a rustling against the phone, like the sound of a soft pillow or a child's cheek, rubbing against the receiver. Timothy must be nodding, Stan thinks.

TIMOTHY: "Yup, I'm fine. I'm in my room. Sittin' on the floor, under my desk so I don't wake up my mom. I've got her cell phone. Maybe she'd be mad."

STAN: "Are you not supposed to use your mom's cell phone, Timothy?"

More rubbing sounds. Shaking his head, perhaps.

TIMOTHY: "No, I can use her phone. It's paid by her company, and she says I can use it. It's not that. It's just that it's still dark out and I'm supposed to be sleeping. She doesn't like it when I don't sleep. She gets mad at me."

STAN: "Yeah. Moms are like that."

The computer panel flashes red: Stan's cue to get back on air.

STAN: "I gotta go, Timothy. I've got this radio show, I've . . . "

TIMOTHY: "Yup, I know. That's why I called. I want to tell you how I think I'll die."

STAN: "Well, I . . ."

TIMOTHY: "I'll wait."

Stan looks at the receiver. His cue button

flashes again, like an alarm.

STAN: "Okay. Okay. I'll get you on the line."

He transfers the phone line to the digital feed.

STAN (to himself): "Probably just wants to hear his own voice on his laptop."

The Temple Man signature flourish rumbles and squawks, cello over piano.

STAN: "This is Stan, your Temple Man. Live at five. Looking into our deadliest dreams in the Dying Hour. We have a special guest tonight, a master Timothy on the phone, awake in these wee hours. Timothy. My man. What are you up to?"

TIMOTHY: "I'm talking on the phone."

STAN: "Yes, you are."

TIMOTHY: "I'm supposed to be sleeping."

STAN: "Yes, that's what people your age usually do at this hour of the morning. Heck, it's what people MY age usually do at this hour of the morning!"

A big, warm laugh.

TIMOTHY: "Wull, I wanted to tell you how I think I'll die."

STAN: "This is the Dying Hour. So go ahead, Tim."

TIMOTHY: "Timothy, please."

STAN: "Okay, sorry Timothy. I just thought you might like Tim better. It sounds older, in a way."

TIMOTHY: "I do like Tim better. But my dad wants me to be called Timothy. Not Tim. So you better call me Timothy."

STAN: "Is your dad up at this hour, Timothy? Would he know if I called you Tim? It could be our little secret."

TIMOTHY: "I think he'd know. I don't know how, but I just think he'd know."

STAN: "Hmm. Well. How old are you, Tim. Timothy."

TIMOTHY: "I'm nine."

STAN: "Nine! Okay then. One year older than the age of reason . . . at least in 1852!"

Stan has to work a bit to push out his laughter. The pepperoni stick isn't going down so well.

TIMOTHY: "What does that mean?"

STAN: "The age of reason?"

TIMOTHY: "Yeah. What does it mean?"

STAN: "It means that a long time ago, people thought that a kid . . . a person, had reached the age where they could use reason—use logic, and common sense—by the time they were eight, and so everyone thought they could make all their own decisions. Be an adult . . . "

TIMOTHY: "Like a grown-up?"

STAN: " . . . like a grown-up. At eight years old. And you're nine."

TIMOTHY: "Huh."

STAN: "So probably, at nine years old, you could make up your own mind about what you would like to be called. If you prefer to be called Tim, then I could call you Tim. It wouldn't hurt even if your dad knew. Even if he thought the name Timothy was better."

TIMOTHY: "Huh. I don't think so, though. My mom, she calls me Tim sometimes, but only when my dad isn't around. Like if he's out of town for a few days. He doesn't like it so she never calls me anything but Timothy if he's in town. I think she knows he could find out. I don't know how but I think somehow he knows."

Stan taps a pen on the table. The plastic tip makes a hard, dull sound against the table top that seems too sharp against the quiet.

STAN: "Hmm. Well. Still, I could call you Tim . . ."

TIMOTHY: "Please don't. Please don't. He'll know somehow, and I don't like it when he does. Please just call me Timothy. It's alright that way. I don't mind. Timothy's an alright name. It's just that, wull, I feel like I have to stand up straight when my dad calls me Timothy. Like if my hair's sticking out, I gotta fix it, get it to lay down right. But he's my dad, and I gotta respect him."

STAN: "Okay, okay, I see your point, Timothy. I do. You are a man at—beyond!—the age of reason, and you can decide. If Timothy works for you and for your dad, then Timothy is who you shall be."

TIMOTHY: "Thanks. I just don't want dad

to hear me and get up. You know, if the knowing somehow wakes him up."

STAN: "Would he be mad, if he knew you were up?"

TIMOTHY: "Um. I don't know. Um. Maybe. I don't know. He'd just tell my mom, I guess."

STAN: "Would your mom be mad at you for being up, Timothy?"

TIMOTHY: "Yup. I tol' you that already, mister Temple. She'd be mad. She'd say I was going to be tired all day in school."

STAN: "That's probably true, Tim. Timothy. You probably should get back to bed. Too much coffee keeping you up?"

TIMOTHY: "What?"

STAN: "Never mind. Never mind. So, Timothy, what's worrying you tonight?"

TIMOTHY: "I want to tell you how I'm going to die, because you said you want to know how people think they're gonna die. And I think I know my way."

STAN: "The floor's all yours, Tim."

TIMOTHY: "Timothy."

STAN: "Timothy. Sorry."

TIMOTHY: "M'kay. I think I'm gonna die 'cause someone's gonna come through my bedroom window and take me away and beat me up and hurt me and scare me until I die from being so scared by them."

The line is quiet, but Timothy can be heard

breathing hard. Deep, quick breaths.

STAN: "My. That's really a scary idea, Timothy."

TIMOTHY: "Yup."

More heavy breathing.

STAN: "Are you trying not to cry, Timothy."

TIMOTHY: "Uh huh."

More quiet. More breathing. Muffled sounds, like a pyjama sleeve wiping across a face and phone, like the bow of a violin.

TIMOTHY: "But I'm not gonna cry because only girls cry once they're big enough, and I do not like to cry."

STAN: "Ah."

TIMOTHY: "And my dad would know if I cried, and that . . . that wouldn't be good."

STAN: "What would happen if your dad knew that you had cried, Tim."

TIMOTHY: "Timothy."

The word comes out in a near whisper.

STAN: "Timothy. What would happen. Would your dad hurt you?"

TIMOTHY: "You don't know my dad. I don't know if he would hurt me. He would just get stern. That's all."

STAN: "Hmm."

Stan wants to sound lighthearted. The pepperoni stick is stuck somewhere in his gullet. He pulls out the silver flask and takes a dry swig.

Timothy says nothing. He just breathes,

deeply and rapidly. But the pace of his breathing is slowing.

STAN: "I'm not so sure that you're going to die that way, Timothy. Probably not."

TIMOTHY: "You don't think so?"

The child sounds so earnest.

STAN: "No, I don't think so. Where's your bedroom in your house, Timothy? Are you there now?"

TIMOTHY: "Yes. Why? Why do you want to know? Are you . . . you're not . . . oh!"

More rapid breathing on the line.

STAN: "Timothy, Timothy. No worries, my little man, no worries. I just wanted to help you think this through. I mean, it's very unlikely that you would get taken from your own house. Isn't that right, listeners? Give us a call, and let's lay our Timothy's fears to rest on this one. And while we wait for inspiration from above (and below and beyond and beneath and betwixt) we'll ride the wave of a little country rock . . ."

Stan lets the music move away from him.

STAN: "Timothy? You still there?"

TIMOTHY: "Uh huh."

STAN: "Okay. We'll be back on the line in a minute, okay?"

TIMOTHY: "M'kay."

Stan saves the line with the push of a phone peg, and gets up to rub his face and pace. He skirts the table, back and forth, for a few long strides. He stops, turns to the glass window panels of the unused technical booth, and rubs the day's new beard growth, hard, as if washing himself clean. In the dim light, he looks much older than his thirty-two years. He pushes the phone peg again to speak on air to the kid.

STAN: "Hey, Timothy. I've got an idea. How 'bout you call me every night when you wake up, okay? We can talk a bit, and maybe that will help you get back to sleep."

TIMOTHY: "Can we talk softly?"

STAN: "Yes. You can talk as softly as you want. And you know what might help, too? Turn off your laptop when you call, so you don't get feedback. That's the screechy, confusing noise you hear sometimes when you're on the phone, at the same time that your voice comes through the laptop. 'Kay?"

TIMOTHY: "M'kay. I think that would be okay. I don't think I would get into any trouble for that. Not if I'm safe in my room, under my desk. I think that would be fine."

STAN: "Okay. Timothy, we have a deal then. You are quite the little man."

TIMOTHY: "Mmm. Do I have to stay on the line now? I think my mom is getting up to pee."

STAN: "Oh."

Both Stan and Timothy wait, listening hard.

TIMOTHY: "It's okay, I think it was just the cat."

Both Stan and Timothy suck in and release a deep breath, simultaneously.

STAN: "Okay, we have a plan. You'll call every night when you wake up, and we'll talk. That works for you?"

TIMOTHY: "Yup. Can I go back to bed now? My head is starting to hurt, and I'm getting cold."

STAN: "Yes. You can go back to bed, Timothy. We'll talk tomorrow night, okay? You can tell me more about your dream."

TIMOTHY: "It's not a dream, mister Temple. I just know. It's how I'm gonna die."

Stan hears the child's voice get tight again, but then Timothy yawns.

STAN: "You'll be alright, Timothy. I promise. Now get to bed, and sleep tight."

Timothy's yawn pulsates—he must be nodding into the phone.

TIMOTHY: "M'kay I gotta go now. It's almost morning. I can sleep now. But wait, mister Temple. You should know somethin'."

STAN: "Hmm?"

TIMOTHY: "You sound just like God."

Stan pushes a smirking breath through his nose.

STAN: "I do?"

TIMOTHY: "Yup. Just like my mom said. G'night, mister Temple."

STAN: "It's God to you, son," *Stan jokes, but the connection has been broken. The empty line buzzes at Stan, like a cranky wasp.*

STAN: "Huh. Well, ain't that a gift from heaven."

The telephone lines spring to life.

'Bring!'

'Bring!' 'Bring!'

STAN: "We're still live, folks, and the lines are hoppin'! This is Stan, the one and only Temple Man, and tonight we are saving the world. Caller one, what's your name, please?"

The studio grows dark.

ACT I, Scene 2
Confession

The studio is dark. The lights come up slowly to reveal Stan, who looks like he hasn't slept in days. He is poorly shaven, and his hair is unkempt. His sits slumped in a chair with his elbows leaning on the table, one hand in the tangle of his hair. The small silver flask sits on the table, glowing red in the flicker of caller lights.

STAN: "Line one. You have reached Stan, the Temple Man. At your service. May I ask your name, please?"

FEMALE CALLER: "Mary Lou. From County Line three."

STAN: "Nice to hear from you, Mary Lou. And what would you like to share with the world tonight, my dear."

The smile is gone from Stan's voice, and he has to stifle a yawn.

FEMALE CALLER: "I'm calling about that kid, Timmy . . . "

STAN: "You mean Timothy."

FEMALE CALLER: "Yeah, that kid that called the other night. I've been thinking about him."

STAN: "Me too," *Stan says. His eyebrows lift and his eyes skim over the tabletop, finding nothing of interest to perch upon.*

FEMALE CALLER: "Well, I think the kid needs help. Like he has a mental health issue. I mean, what's a six year old . . ."

STAN: "He's nine. Age of reason, and beyond."

FEMALE CALLER: "So, nine, and he can't sleep and is calling in to an adult radio show. I mean, something is wrong. It's so obvious. Like, maybe the kid's been abandoned."

Stan bobs his head, considering the possibility.

STAN: "Could be. But then again, he had his mother's cell phone."

FEMALE CALLER: "Well, he SAID it was his mother's cell phone. But WAS it?"

STAN: "Good point. Maybe he rolled some old street bum for the phone. Is that what you mean?"

FEMALE CALLER: "Well, yeah. Maybe. He coulda."

Stan bobs his head again. He lifts his full cheek off its perch in his palm, and straightens.

STAN: "You have a point, Mary Lou. We really don't know anything about our Timothy. And he hasn't called back, so we can't fill in the blanks. But my gut tells me that . . ."

The phone rings. Stan pivots forward from the hip joint, to see that the digital ID window reads 'Unknown'.

STAN: "Well, speak of the devil. Timothy!!"

TIMOTHY: "Shhh!! Mister Temple, you said you'd speak softly."

STAN: "Well, technically, Timothy, I said YOU could speak softly, but still, it's great to hear from you. Thank you, Mary Lou from County Line three. We'll see if we can solve that mystery of yours. But first, a little Musak to put us in the mood for contemplating our own childhood navels . . . give a listen to: 'If You Want My Body And You Think I'm Sexy' by the Boston Pops . . ." *Then privately, he says* "Timothy! How are you, son! You haven't called in days. You must be sleeping better."

Stan lets his voice boom.

TIMOTHY: "No. I just couldn't get my mom's cell phone, 'cause she's been away. She went to stay with my aunt, who lives a couple hours away."

STAN: "Aah."

TIMOTHY: "Yeah. She came back, though."

STAN: "Hmm. That's good, I'll bet."

TIMOTHY: "Oh yeah."

STAN: "Are you ready to go live? That means get on the air. You know, speak so that people can hear you over their radios. And laptops."

TIMOTHY: "Sure."

STAN: "Alright, my man, we are ON IT. Ladies and lovers, the moment is now. We have Timothy, the mystery caller, back on the line after a two day absence. How's life treating you, Timothy?"

TIMOTHY: "Good."

STAN: "Good. Glad to hear that."

Several lights flash on the telephone desk-set, twinkling like Christmas lights. Stan's smile broadens.

STAN: "Timothy, you might be surprised to know that many, many people are interested in what you've got to say. A lot of people have been wondering about why you called, and about what we can do to help you."

TIMOTHY: "I don't know."

STAN: "Well, of course you don't know, Timothy. If you knew how to help yourself you wouldn't be calling, right?"

TIMOTHY: "I guess."

STAN: "Are you cold, Timothy? You sound a bit far away. Is your mouth close enough to the phone."

TIMOTHY: "Just trying to whisper, is all. I don't want my mom and dad to wake up. They've been fighting a lot lately and I don't like it."

Silence. Lights blink wildly on the phone.

STAN: "Does that scare you, Tim?"

TIMOTHY: "Timothy, please. Yeah, I guess. I just don't like it. I want it to stop."

STAN: "I think all our listeners could relate to that, Timothy. Many of us can remember times when our parents fought. It doesn't feel very good. You don't know what will happen next."

TIMOTHY: "Like divorce."

Stan nods. His face grows grave. He switches on an extra light overhead, which beads down on him in a cold, white wash. He rubs his forehead hard with a forearm, and lifts the small tarnished silver flask to his mouth, only to find the flask empty. He tosses it down without putting the cap back on.

Across the table from him, Stan sees a play of ghostly images on the glass window screen of the sound booth.

STAN'S DAD: "You're not wearing that, are you, Gail?"

STAN'S MAMA: "Why wouldn't I wear this, Frank. It's perfectly fetching, isn't it, Stan? Mama's happy boy?"

STAN'S DAD: "That dress makes you look fat. Actually, everything makes you look fat. In fact, maybe we shouldn't go out at all."

STAN'S DAD takes a swig from the flask in his breast pocket.

STAN'S MAMA: "Oh Frank, do you have to do that?"

STAN'S DAD: "Get off my back, Gail. I'm just a bit uptight. You know how I hate these business socials."

STAN'S MAMA: "You're just worried about what your boss's wife is going to think about me. Don't you worry. She'll love me. Besides, there's nothing we can do about it now. We have to go. And I look fine. Right, Stan, my happy boy? Aren't we the perfect family?"

Stan stares warily, watching his mother for clues, his face serious.

STAN'S MAMA: "Now look, Frank, look how you've upset our Stan. And he's such a little peach. Everything should be just right for our happy little peach."

STAN'S PAPA: "You're making a brat out of him, Gail. A real faggot. I don't want any son of mine to be a pansy. Now change your damn clothes and let's get going."

STAN'S DAD takes another swig. He puts the flask back in his pocket. Stan's parents fade into the backdrop.

STAN: "But everybody fights, Timothy. It means nothing. It's just what families do."

The phone lights flicker wildly.

Timothy is silent.

STAN: "Let's take a caller, Timothy. Caller on line four, what's your name?"

WOMAN CALLER: "Hello Stan, this is

Trish, from West Lake. I just want to tell Timothy that he's a very brave boy for trying to get help."

TIMOTHY: "I . . ."

STAN: "He hasn't actually asked for help, Trish. We might be jumping the gun a bit with that. Caller, line three. What do you have to say?"

MALE CALLER: "Hey Timbo."

TIMOTHY: "Hullo."

MALE CALLER: "You've got to stand up to your old man about your name, boy. If you don't, he'll run your life forever. Ask Stevie. I know. My old man's a monster. Won't let me do things my own way at all. I'm fifty, an' I'm STILL rakin' his leaves and doin' his jobs around the house. Puttin' up with his bullshit. An' I'm sick of it."

STAN: "Thank you, Steve. Call six."

FEMALE CALLER: "Amanda, here. I just wanted to tell Timothy that he is being very bold in getting up and using his mother's cell-o-phone without her permission . . ."

TIMOTHY: "But she says I can use it! I promise she does!"

Timothy's voice zooms high, off the charts.

STAN: "It's okay, Timothy. This is just one woman's opinion."

FEMALE CALLER: "Bold! That's what this is. This child should NOT be up!"

STAN: "Thank you, Amanda. Next caller . . ."

MALE CALLER: "Why don't we let the kid talk a bit more, and see what he has to say. Never know. We could learn some-pin."

Stan nods.

STAN: "What do you think, Timothy? Are you up for a chat?"

TIMOTHY: "Okay. As long as we talk quiet."

STAN: "Yessir. Stay tuned, folks, as Stan, The Temple Man gets close to Timothy, right after this commercial message."

A red light bleeps on Stan's keyboard. He hunkers down, looking straight at the microphone hovering in front of his nose, as if it were Timothy's face.

STAN: "Timothy. You ready?"

TIMOTHY: "Yup. I just got a blanket, so I don't get cold. And I put some socks on, too."

STAN: "Okay, we're live in three, two . . ."

Stan inserts a musical crescendo into the space between Timothy and him.

STAN: "Welcome back, all you night-riders. You are with Stan, the Temple Man, exploring this sleeping city's secrets. We have Timothy, a nine year old insomniac with us . . ."

TIMOTHY: "Um . . ."

STAN: "An insomniac is a person who can't sleep, Timothy. You're having trouble sleeping, right?"

TIMOTHY: "Oh. Yeah."

STAN: "So, what's on your mind? The last time we talked, you were thinking about someone getting into your room at night. Now, that's not very likely, Timothy. First off, is your house a two storey house, or a bungalow?"

TIMOTHY: "Um. . . I . . ."

STAN: "Do you have to go up stairs to go to bed, Timothy?"

TIMOTHY: "Yeah. Thirteen stairs, plus two around the corner."

STAN: "Okay. Sounds like an old house, with high ceilings then, for all those stairs. So you're very high up off the ground, if you look out your window, right?"

TIMOTHY: "Yeah. Do you want me to look out the window now, mister Temple?"

STAN: "No, you don't have to do that, son. I just want you to realize that it would be very hard for someone to climb up the side of your house and get through your window."

TIMOTHY: "But they could. There are ladders. My neighbour, he has a big ladder and he can get right up on to his own roof."

STAN: "Yes, but you would hear someone climbing up to your window. And then once he got in, he'd have to take you back down the ladder. And you would fight, right?"

TIMOTHY: "Well, yes, but then I might fall, and that would be so scary. Maybe I wouldn't fight at all."

The child's voice starts to waiver.

STAN: "Okay, but you would fight so hard before he got you through the window that I'll bet your mom and dad would hear you."

TIMOTHY: "Um. Yeah. They would, I

bet."

STAN: "And you could spread yourself out like a starfish, so that he couldn't even GET you through the window, even if he pulled really hard."

Timothy giggles.

TIMOTHY: "Ha! Yeah, my cat did that one time, when she was just a kitten. She stepped in her own poop, so we had to wash her paws, and when we tried to stick her in the bathroom sink she just went all stiff, like a big star. Even her FINGERS went stiff! She was sticking out all over! My mom couldn't even get her in the sink. She just wouldn't bend! It was so funny!"

Timothy giggles. The sound spills all over the studio, bouncing off the hard glass walls. Stan beams in the light from his computer screen, his face as big and white as the Westclox face behind him.

STAN: "See? If a little kitten can do that, just think what a strong boy of nine could do to keep from going out a window."

Timothy settles down, and in a single breath is as grim as ever.

TIMOTHY: "Yeah, but I wouldn't have to go through the window. Someone could just tape my mouth shut—my mom uses duct tape and it sticks on everything—and then they could tie me up and take me down the stairs and right out the front door."

Stan's smile fades.

STAN: "That COULD happen, but it WON'T. This is just a bad dream for you, Timothy. It's scary, but it's not real."

Timothy hiccups. Short tattered breaths pummel the receiver, magnified in the studio darkness.

TIMOTHY: "Wull, it feels real."

STAN: "Where did you get this idea, Timothy?"

TIMOTHY: "My dad. He tol' me about a girl that was stolen from her house. He saw it on the news. When they found her, she was dead."

Stan rubs his face.

STAN: "That's too bad, Timothy. That's a very sad story. I'm sorry you got to hear it. Well, listeners, I am looking to you for some feedback, here. What do you say?"

The lines on his phone set fire up.

MALE CALLER: "The Dad's an asswipe . . ."

FEMALE CALLER: "Poor little tyke. Someone ought to call the Children's Aid."

MAN CALLER: "I heard that news story too, it was horrendahssss . . ."

WOMAN CALLER: "He could try some ginger in milk. That will put him to sleep like a baby!"

STAN: "Well, Timothy. How 'bout some ginger milk. Hmm?"

TIMOTHY: "I don't like milk. It makes me want to spit. From my throat."

STAN: "Ha! Okay then. Let's move along.

What else do we know about you? We know you're having trouble sleeping. We know your name is Timothy, and that your dad wants people to call you Timothy, not Tim. So. How about we talk about your dad, Timothy. Is he a little hard on you?"

TIMOTHY: "Wull, I don't know. Yeah. Maybe. But he kinda treats me like he treats everybody else. He just doesn't, wull, get happy, much, about stuff. It's like you're always in school with him. And no matter how hard you try or how many right answers you get, you always get some wrong, and you gotta walk around with big red exes on you."

STAN: "Mmm. I think a lot of our listeners tonight could identify with that, Timothy."

TIMOTHY: "Yeah. Maybe that's what dads are. Kinda . . . um . . ."

STAN: "Mean?"

TIMOTHY: "Well, not mean, really. Just, um, stiff? Like you gotta do stuff right around 'em. Or they get mad. You gotta respect 'em. Different than other people. You gotta respect 'em even when they do the things they tell you YOU can't do."

STAN: "Aah. Now you're getting somewhere, Timothy. What does your dad do that he tells you *you* can't do?"

TIMOTHY: "Mmmm. Wull, like, he says I can't stay up late watching TV, and he does. Or like, I can't put my feet on the furniture, but he does. Or talking back to my mom. Or like telling her to shut up."

STAN: "Ooooh. Yup. That's a good one. I mean, why would you tell your mom to shut up, anyway, right? There's probably a better way to say that, a way that doesn't sound so angry. You know, like: Please stop talking."

TIMOTHY: "Mmmhmm."

STAN: "Alright, listeners. The lines are open again. Call in to tell us what YOUR dad does, that you weren't allowed to do. We'll compare bruises. Get your dialing fingers going to 1-800-YOU-TELL. And while you're fuming about past injustices, have a listen to 'R-E-S-P-E-C-T'."

Stan lets the song play out loud.

STAN: "I'll be right back, Timothy, okay. Just taking a bit of a break."

TIMOTHY: "M'kay. I'll go pee."

Stan gets up to pace. He shakes his arms and legs like an athlete, preparing for a run. He doesn't dare look at the glass wall.

STAN'S MOM appears before him, and he stops dead. Her hands are clasped near her full face, and she brings them down, still joined, and looks adoringly at Stan.

STAN: "Mom. Don't. Okay?"

STAN'S MOM: "Oh where's my little happy man? Your father's just in one of his moods. He'll feel better soon. He just had too many peanuts."

She fades, and reappears on the other side of the room, looking behind her, urging him with her pudgy palms downward to stay away, to stay quiet.

STAN'S MOM: "Stan," *she says in a stage whisper.* "Stan! Keep it down. Your dad has one of his headaches. We don't want to wake him, now do we? I know it's two in the afternoon, but he didn't sleep very well last night. You know how those Parkses get under his skin. I don't know why we have them over. And they drink so much! So please, Stan, keep your music down."

Stan stops to watch her. He rubs his face, burying his features beneath his beefy hands. She reappears at his shoulder.

STAN'S MOM: "C'mon, Stan. My happy boy. Just this one time. I just really want to see that movie, and your dad's not up to it. Oh, you know how he is. The game is on. He's settled in already. Just this once? You can drive, and I'll buy you popcorn. It'll be fun, you'll see. And I'd be so proud to be out on the town with my own little man. What do you say, Stan? Why not? Where's the harm?"

STAN'S MOM retreats, and he is alone in the studio. 'R-E-S-P-E-C-T' booms in the background. Stan's arms hang long at his sides.

TIMOTHY: "Mister Temple?" *Timothy is whispering.*

Stan bolts for his computer station, addressing the mike as if it were Timothy himself.

STAN: "Yes, Timothy, I'm here."

TIMOTHY: "I'm back from my pee. I just wanted you to know."

STAN: "Okay, we'll be on in a second. Did you wash your hands, son?"

TIMOTHY: "Um. M'kay, I'll be back in a second."

STAN: "Hurry, man."

As the last few bars of the song dissolve, Stan presses his lips to the mike. He brings out his richest, deepest tones.

STAN: "You are in the belly of the beast, all you lovers and loners. We are looking into the eye of our own personal storm: our fathers. So, listeners, what stories do you have to tell to keep our Timothy company through this long, sleepless night?"

CALLER ONE: "My dad used to get to eat first, no matter how late he was or how hungry we were. Even when we had company over."

CALLER TWO: "Pops always got the best cut of meat. AND the best spot on the couch. And one of us kids had to be his remote— remember? Back in the day when you had to switch the channels by hand?"

CALLER THREE: "Got to use all the hot water in the tank, for a bath."

CALLER FOUR: "Had his own bathroom. And we were five girls!"

CALLER FIVE: "Made me lick his dick, the asshole. Christ!"

STAN: "Woe-hoe! Daddy!"

The push of a button inserts an urgent police siren call.

Stan shakes his head hard, letting his jowls flap loudly.

STAN: "Emergency, emergency! Stan the Temple Man is declaring a truce! Can anybody help out there? Caller six. Keep it clean, please. There's a kid on the line."

CALLER SIX: "Stan, Stan, you're playing with fire here, buddy."

STAN: "No kidding. Anybody have a hose?"

CALLER SIX: "This is Paul Somers. I work the twenty-four-seven telephone help line, and this stuff you're delving into is way over your head, bud. You need schooling to start playing around with memories. You'll dig up all kinds of dirt you won't know how to handle. Clear out now, while you can. That's my advice, bud."

STAN: "Yes, yes, I can see how we might be getting in over our heads, here."

CALLER SIX: "Any listeners who need to talk to a qualified professional should call 1-866-GET-HELP; that's 1-866-438-4357. There's someone on staff 'round the clock. Twenty four seven."

STAN: "Thanks, Paul. Paul Somers of the Twenty-four-seven Help Hotline. All you folks out there with baggage that needs putting down—caller number five is my first draft pick—

please call 1-866-438-4357, also known as 1-866-GET-HELP. Call NOW. You've freaked ME out. So you must be BLEEDING. That's 1-866-GET-HELP. And now a commercial break, with this special message from Fenkels Ford. If that doesn't sober us up, nothing will."

Stan silences the blaring trumpets of the Fenkels Ford ad, and cradles his head in his hands. He fishes around for his metal flask and holds it to his forehead, then to each cheek, before turning the empty flask upside down.

The phone rings. Stan glances at the caller ID window, and groans. He picks up the receiver.

STAN: "Mister Edwards. Ernie. I know what you're calling about. I'm doing my best to . . . Oh. This isn't about the content. Oh. OH." *Stan laughs.* "Okay, my apologies to Fenkels. I was just trying to keep it light. I'll run his ad an extra half dozen times. Okay, a dozen times. Send him my apologies, please. I'm sorry. It won't happen again. Gotcha. Thanks. Sorry he woke you, sir. Goodnight."

Stan replaces the receiver, hangs his head and laughs into the moon of his belly.

He flicks Timothy's phone line to 'live'.

STAN: "Timothy." *He says the word loudly, booming like the voice of God.*

TIMOTHY: "Huh?"

STAN: "Sorry about some of that."

TIMOTHY: "Yeah. Yuck."

STAN: "You said it, man. Whoo! You

okay?"

TIMOTHY: "I guess."

STAN: "You tired yet?"

TIMOTHY: "Wull, yeah but, I can't sleep."

STAN: "Okay man, we're with ya. Keep hangin' in there. Alright folks. We're back on line. Do we dare to try this again?"

Stan's control panel lights up.

STAN: "Line one, you're up. Be kind, please."

LINE ONE: "Kind. Yeah. But we should be kind for that caller five, too, the one with the pedophile father."

STAN: "Pedophile INCESTUOUS father."

LINE ONE: "Yeah. Where's the kindness in that, eh? Using some kid as a kind of sex toy. It's not right."

STAN: "Well, obviously, but cheez, we've got a kid on the line tonight—one that's scared to go to bed. Can't we tone it down, just a bit? I agree that caller five deserves our collective and individual empathy; it's just a matter of context, man. Stan the Temple Man cannot put a positive spin on EVERYTHING. Next caller, please."

LINE TWO: "That last guy was right. You've gotta give sympathy where sympathy is due. I mean, can you imagine? You own dad? It's . . ."

STAN: "Okay, we got it, already. The dad in this case is obviously twisted. But hey, maybe there's some kind of explanation. Like maybe the man was bombed at the time or something . . ."

The phone lines light up like fireflies!

LINE THREE: "Yur right! Guys make mistakes! It's not your fault, man, if you can't remember what ya done. Ya gotta cut some slack."

LINE FOUR: "I cannot believe that you would even entertain the thought that inebriation might excuse this kind of abominable behaviour. A child is a child is a child, and there is no room for sexual exploitation of such an innocent creature. That is the most infantile approach to a complicated problem that I've ever heard and . . ."

STAN: "My hands are up, I surrender, deservedly chastised. The personal safety police are on patrol and rightly so. All of us are restless tonight. Whoo! I'm taking it in the chops. Now boys and girls, what I meant is: hey. Sometimes a guy (or a gal) takes in more booze than anticipated. You know? Like maybe you're not taking as much care as you should to keep a tally. I'm not saying that booze excuses you, most certainly not from something heinous like child abuse, and yet I've heard even intelligent, educated, capable people say it—when you've had too much to drink and you don't remember what you did, can it really count against you? Can you really be blamed?"

LINE FIVE: "Alcohol's a sin, brother. Plain and simple. Like cigarettes. Gets you in where you don't wanta go."

LINE SIX: "'Dat old story dat you were not in charge of yourself and so den you can't be guilty is a lot of hooey!'"

LINE SEVEN: "Alcoholism is a disease, and we should all feel sympathy for someone who's sick. Alcoholism is like cancer. It eats you up and you'll do anything to stop it. You're not yourself. You can't be held accountable, just like if you were in pain and you broke into a pharmacy just to steal pain medication, then you shouldn't go to jail for that neither. You shouldn't be blamed for anything you do when you're drunk. It's not your fault if you can't help it."

STAN: "Next caller, you're up."

CALLER ONE: "That's a load of crap!"

CALLER TWO: "If you've got AIDS and you give it to someone else, then you're considered criminally negligent. Same kinda story here. You get drunk and you hurt someone? Criminally negligent. Guilty as charged."

CALLER THREE: "We've solved this whole problem by legalizing marijuana. Nobody who uses pot has ever been accused of screwing their own kid."

TIMOTHY: "Mister Temple. Mister Temple, can I butt in, please."

STAN: "You've got the air, Timothy. Thank God."

TIMOTHY: "It does so count if you're

drunk."

STAN: "What do you know about being drunk, Timothy."

Stan picks up the flask from his desk, and rummages around until he finds the cap.

TIMOTHY: "Wull, I don't know much but my cousin says that being drunk is like spinning around and around a bunch of times until you feel sick and can't see straight, and when you try to walk you go all wiggly and zig zag. So I know what it feels like."

Stan teeters his head, left to right, right to left, considering this reasoning.

TIMOTHY: "And being drunk doesn't TRANSFORM you into a 'nother person. That transforming junk, that's all just pretend. It's not real, you know. It's not like if I eat a lot of pizza until I'm sick, or like, spin around a lot until I can't see straight, that I TRANSFORM into a 'nother person. It's still me."

STAN: "Not the same thing."

STAN'S MAMA and STAN'S DAD appear behind him: Stan sees their reflection in the glass wall of the studio.

STAN'S MAMA (calmly): "Now, Frank, you don't have to do that, Frank. I never talked ill of you. I would never do that."

STAN'S DAD: "You called me a fool, Gail. You did it with your eyes, the way . . . the way you looked at me like . . . like I'm silly. You're just . . . jussa bitch, Gail. You always make me look bad.

If I hadna married you, I'd be . . . so much better. You ruin ever-thing, Gail. Ever-thing."

STAN'S DAD pushes his MAMA up against the wall, his elbow across her neck.

STAN'S MAMA (struggling): "Frank, please. This isn't necessary. It didn't happen like that."

STAN'S DAD: "Never shoulda married you, you bitch. Should kill you, that's what. One of these days, I'll just wipe you right off the world."

Stan turns toward the figures. He's taken a flashlight from the work station, and points the harsh beam directly at them. The figures of both mother and father are caught in the light, features drowning in the overwhelming light, shadows growing and stretching like spider legs across the walls and ceiling. A play of red and blue lights wash over their outlines, pushing them back into the wall, into the shadows, erasing them from view. Stan turns to see emergency lights play across the length of glass that cuts through the studio. And the vision fades.

The phone lines are going crazy.

TIMOTHY: "Mister Temple. Are you still there?"

STAN: "Yes. I am here, Timothy. I was just remembering. You're not quite right about being drunk. People do transform. The person you know can become a whole different person. They can do things they would never do sober."

TIMOTHY: "Wull that's just dumb."

STAN (after a pause): "Maybe. But it's real. Or maybe it's not the booze that forces the change: maybe it's people. Women. Especially women who don't drink. What is it about forty year old women that makes men so crazy? What gets into women that they just won't cut a guy any breaks? That they just start asking for it? How 'bout we get some listener comments about this. The mike is yours, fine listeners. Call in with your views on alcohol and its place in our homes and in our lies."

TIMOTHY: "Did you say 'lies', mister Temple? Like in 'fibs'? Stuff that's not true?"

STAN: "No, Timothy, I said 'lives.' Lines are open again. And, they're lighting up. We have an S. Menley here. What's your story, Menley?"

LADY CALLER: "Ms. Menley, if you please. I want to have a word with you, Stan Templeman, and that word is JERK. You wanta know what happens to forty year old women? They just can't lie down no more. They just can't take no more abuse and they gotta speak up, they gotta defend themselves, even if their chops get busted. My old man, my husband, he fucked my best friend's brother! It went on for FIVE YEARS . . ."

STAN: "Language, please, or . . ."

LADY CALLER: "It's the middle of the night! Who listens?"

STAN: "Timothy."

LADY CALLER: "Okay. That's true. I'm sorry for my bad language, Timothy."

TIMOTHY: " 'sokay, ma'am."

LADY CALLER: "You're very polite, Timothy. You're obviously being very well raised. I'm sorry I used the eff word in front of you. But my point stands, Stan Templeman. Only JERKS blame women for their bad behaviour."

The line clicks off.

TIMOTHY: "She sounded mad."

STAN: "Yup."

TIMOTHY: "I heard that eff word before, it's okay. It's different, the way that lady said it, though. I never heard it like that before. But I know what it means. Makes me feel kinda crawly, though. That whole idea. I don't like to think about it. Especially about my mom and dad. Uck."

STAN: "I think you've stumbled on a universal truth, young man. Marital sex, especially between your own mother and father, is very definitely 'uck'."

TIMOTHY: "Yeah. I don't think my mom would do that, anyway. Maybe my mom and dad never did . . . sex. Do you think that's possible, mister Temple?"

Stan rubs his chin. A smile builds behind his eyes, but never emerges.

STAN: "I'm sorry to tell you, Timothy, my son, but I can pretty much guarantee that your mother and father have had sex. You are the proof."

TIMOTHY: "Oh yeah. I knew that. Huh! But do you think they do now?"

STAN: "I would have no way of knowing that, Timothy. Maybe they do, maybe they don't."

TIMOTHY: "I hope they don't. Not just because it's ucky. But because . . ."

STAN: "Yes?"

TIMOTHY: "Wull, I was just wondering. I mean, I know this isn't what most kids want, but, wull, I been thinking that maybe it would be better if my mom and dad broke up."

STAN: "Is that what's happening, Timothy? Is that why you can't sleep? Is that why your mom was gone to your aunt's house for a few days?"

TIMOTHY: "Dunno. I don't think so. Nobody's said anything to me. Mom keeps telling me she wants me to respect my dad, so I don't think anything's happening. What I mean is, I WANT it to happen."

STAN: "You want your parents to divorce?"

TIMOTHY: "Yeah. I just think maybe it would be easier if my dad didn't live here anymore. Like maybe it would be, y'know, quieter. More fun."

STAN: "And your mom could call you 'Tim'."

TIMOTHY: "Yeah. Like that."

STAN: "Whoo." *Stan pauses, crosses his arms, leans into the mike but doesn't make eye contact with the child it represents.* "You think that's what you want, Timothy? A dad who's gone all the time? A dad you don't get to know any more? A dad your mother takes away from you?"

TIMOTHY: "Yeah. Maybe I do." *He sounds like he might cry.*

The night exists, for a moment, without interruption.

STAN: "Seems like a good time for a plug by our friendly Ford furnisher, Fenkels! Back in a moment, fellow night crawlers."

Stan waits out the ad, simply sitting in the darkness. Timothy breathes on the open line.

STAN: "Keep the calls coming, fellow night crawlers. We've got mysteries to solve. The moment's topic is alcohol and other domestic dangers. Ted B., you're on the line."

GENTLEMAN CALLER: "I just had a kind of sideline to add to this issue of alcohol, Stan. My aunt was an alcoholic—died of liver disease in her fifties. She was always a problem. Never mean. No. But you could never be sure what would happen when she was around. For instance, she fell face first into her plate of pasta at my wedding. At the head table. Nice. Another time, she backed out of her driveway and went right over a cyclist's leg. Got sued for that one. Lost. That kind of thing. But the thing I called about has to do with darkness."

STAN: "Darkness. Please elaborate."

GENTLEMAN CALLER: "Sure thing. It was my mother that pointed this out. See, her place was always dark."

STAN: "Dark."

GENTLEMAN CALLER: "Sure. Dark. For instance, the drapes were always drawn, so no light got in. And all the walls in her house were painted in dark colours. Like brown."

Stan looks over his shoulder at the coffee coloured wall behind him.

GENTLEMAN CALLER: "And so when you went into her house, even if it was bright as day outside, the whole place was kept in darkness. She hardly ever even turned on a light. Only the television screen would be on, so that her face was bathed in this cool, blue light."

Stan rolls his eyes around the darkened room, and settles them on the screen bleeding blue-white light onto his face. He blinks, and stares straight ahead at the vision of his face, a moon-man face, reflected in the facing sound-studio windows.

GENTLEMAN CALLER: "It was very creepy. My mom came up with the theory that alcoholics can't stand the light. It hurts their eyes. Sure. Like a perpetual hangover."

Stan looks around him, sees the shadows moving in, always moving in. He pushes himself away from his work station on the wheels of his desk chair. The chair slides into the darkness, away from the square of light from his computer screen.

In Stan's place, STAN'S DAD appears. He has a beer in one hand and a sandwich in the other.

STAN'S DAD: "Gail! Gail! Get me a refill, will ya? The game is on, and I don't want to miss the next play."

STAN'S MAMA appears on the sidelines. Her plump hands switch her husband's empty beer can for a full one.

STAN'S DAD: "Take this, too," he says, handing her the rest of his sandwich. "It's terrible."

STAN'S MAMA retreats, leaving DAD intent on the game, beer in one hand, little silver flask in the other.

STAN stands in the shadows and looks at his father. He moves toward the work station and watches as his father plays along with the televised game.

STAN: "Timothy. Are you still there?"

TIMOTHY: "Uh huh."

STAN: "Do you think you can sleep now, son?"

TIMOTHY: "My eyes are sandy. Maybe I'll just sit here, and close them for a bit. It'll be morning soon, and then I'll get back in to bed. I can sleep when it's daylight out."

STAN: "Okay. That's good."

TIMOTHY: "Are you tired, mister Temple? You sound tired."

The kid yawns.

STAN: "Naw. I was just remembering. Makes me feel kind of far away."

TIMOTHY: "Like a bad dream. Wull, like you said, mister Temple. It's just a dream. It's not real."

STAN: "It sure feels real. Good night, Timothy. Or good morning. We'll talk to you tomorrow night, then. And for the rest of my devoted listeners: the time has come to shut this wagon down, to dig into the holes we hide in during the day. Thanks for sharing with me, and with Timothy. This is Stan, the Temple Man, over and out."

Stan flicks off the overhead mike.

STAN: "Dad," *he says. His voice doesn't sound so deep, this time.*

STAN'S DAD: "Not now, Stan. Can't you see I'm busy?"

Stan reaches across the screen to put his computer monitor to sleep, and the studio goes dark.

ACT I, Scene 3
Reconciliation

The door to the studio opens abruptly, and bangs against the wall. The stark white hall glows around the figure of Stan Templeman, whose girth blots out most of the light.

The studio is dark, as always. Stan moves into the room, flicks on a light that is anchored to the stem of the microphone hanging down from the ceiling. The light cascades over Stan's angry features.

The rectangle of unforgiving white light from the doorway seems to pulsate in contrast to the darkness. The perfect circle of the Westclox clock glows like a harvest moon. The light over Stan's head rains light in a ragged triangle.

Stan keys in a series of commands at his work station. He looks at the clock. Midnight. He *pushes a button.*

"Good eventide, all you lost souls and sad sisters in our lusty, rusty city tonight," *says Stan's recorded voice.* "Stan your Temple Man is here to soothe your sorrows with a little . . . r and b."

Stan flicks off the light over the microphone and steps back into the rectangle of doorway light, using long, aggressive strides. He slams the door shut behind him.

The recorded voice continues in the pitch dark: "Oh yesss, my flock of late night listeners, the Temple is open. Stan Templeman here, body and soul. It is a murky, murky November night for one and all. But as we all know, anything could happen now that Stan is in the building. Weather shifts in its patterns, the axis of the earth leans infinitesimally to the right or to the left, and you, my dear listeners, tell all. The lines are now open and the night is long . . ."

The words melt into the darkness until all that can be seen or heard is the slow ticking of the clock.

ACT II, Scene 1
Communion

Stan sits in the near-perfect darkness, hugging the mike. His face and upper body are bathed in computer-screen light. His jacket hangs on the chair's backrest, a bright red poppy pinned to the lapel. A half-eaten sandwich sits on the table beside two cans of pop and the small tarnished silver flask, which gleams beneath the shower of light from the mike stem overhead. The door to the white passageway beyond the dimly-lit sound studio remains open; the rectangle of pure white light looks sterile, even hostile. The clock face glows pure white, its hands at three o'clock, and then the circle, and the rectangle doorway, grow dim.

STAN: "The is Stan, the Temple Man, feeling less than cathedral. I'm deep in the belly of this building. Can't see the light, can't find it anywhere. Like Pinocchio in the belly of the whale, Monstro. I'm swallowed up whole. Just waiting for signs of life. Signs of Spring. Callers, help me. Tell me what daylight is like. Phone line one, you're live."

LADY ON LINE 1: "My dog's goin' nuts!"

STAN: "How distressing for you. Is there an emergency vet line you could call? 'Cause I've got nothing for you on that one."

LADY ON LINE 1: "It's gonna storm, that's what that means. When Tippy runs around in circles and jumps up, and bites his own tail, it means there's gonna be a storm. A whopper. Lighting, thunder, the whole shebang."

STAN: "Thanks for the heads up. Maybe it's a good night to be inside, after all. INSIDE the storm. Navel gazing. Trying to find the umbilical cord. Line two, you're up."

MAN ON LINE 2: "Terrible weather. You're missing nothing at all, Stan. Rain. Sleet. Cold. Sucks all around."

WOMAN ON LINE 3: "The wind is angry and howling. Lamenting. Trees are trembling to their roots. There seems to be pain, and trouble afoot."

STAN: "My. That's almost . . . poetic. May I ask who's calling? The line says . . ."

WOMAN ON LINE 3: "My birth name isn't important. It cannot bind my true spirit. This is Madame Orca. I read palms, and tea leaves, and the stars. Tonight, there is change in the air. It may feel frightening, but this reversal is necessary. Cleansing. Good luck with this, Stan. Your temple is crumbling. Brace yourself."

The woman's voice cackles sharply and disconnects with a click.

STAN: "I KNEW I shoulda called in sick."

He laughs quietly, the low rumbling sound puddling miserably in his lap. He reaches for the gleaming silver flask, and takes a swallow.

STAN: "Storm's a brewing. As Shakespeare once said: Toil; foil; boil your troubles. Or something like that. Caller one, your turn. Save me, baby."

CALLER ONE: "I've been thinking about Timothy, the kid who keeps calling in at ungodly hours."

STAN: "Mmhmm."

CALLER ONE: "I've been thinking. He's probably being abused. He's probably from some poor, destitute family, and his father is no doubt hitting him and his mom around. You can hear it in his voice."

STAN: "Hmm. Possible. But then again, he's calling in on his mother's cell phone. And he said he had a laptop—he was picking up our show digitally, over the 'net. So his family can't be all that bad off."

CALLER ONE: "You don't know how these welfare scum waste their money on big screen TVs and beer, instead of paying rent and buying groceries. You can't trust those people. They're takers, not givers."

STAN: "What do you think, listeners out there, battling this stormy night? Do you think Timothy is stuck in a poverty-stricken, abusive home? I've got you lined up. Go, go, go!"

FIRST LINE: "Shit, yes."

SECOND LINE: "Beyond a doubt."

THIRD LINE: "Welfare equals poverty equals lowlifes equals abuse. All goes hand in hand. Any fool knows that. You get a good job, and everything goes good."

FOURTH LINE: "I've got to interrupt, to be the voice of reason, here. This is Doctor Emily David calling. I'm an intern in the city's Emergency Room. I see cases of neglect and abuse all the time, here, and I've studied the subject intensively. In fact I'm working with some of the finest minds in the field on further research into the link between physical development and morbidity . . ."

STAN: "How morbid!"

FOURTH LINE: "I mean the development of disease, caused by neglect and abuse."

STAN: "You mean abuse can actually make you sick."

FOURTH LINE: "Yes. There is a clear causal link. Research has proven it over the past seven decades. Neglect and abuse, in extreme cases, lead to poor motor skills, poor vision, poor hearing . . . there's still more to learn, but there is a link, and a small window within which changes can be made to repair poor biological hardwiring."

STAN: "You mean you could go blind if you came from an abusive home."

FOURTH LINE: "Yes. It's not quite that straightforward, but yes. Or a home where there was neglect. Actually, you wouldn't GO blind, you just wouldn't develop sight normally. But that's not why I called. I just wanted to indicate, clearly, that poverty and abuse and neglect do not go hand in hand. Neglect and abuse exist at all levels of society and income levels. The rich neglect and abuse their children at about the same rate as low-income level households. And middle income families are no different. Abuse and neglect are everywhere."

STAN: "Shit."

FOURTH LINE: "Sorry to burst your bubble."

The line clicks off.

STAN: "Well, that shut us down, now didn't it? Next caller."

CALLER A: "This is Buck, from the Women's Shelter. I'm . . ."

STAN: "Buck! How can you be at a women's shelter, man? I thought guys had to stay AWAY from those places. You can't have the enemy within your walls."

CALLER A: "Hey, not all men are monsters. I'm a feminist, and I'm right where I need to be. I'm corroborating what your caller said. Workin' to keep the bad guys OUT. Not all women are saints; some of them get up to a lot of abusive stuff, but more men do, so there are more women's shelters. In fact, we sometimes get men, but that gets complicated. It's hard for a man who's being abused to find a place to hide safely. But that's another story. That doctor caller is right. The women we see don't all come from the wrong side of the tracks. There are plenty that come from fancy homes. You can see it. Manicures, three hundred dollar haircuts, their kids all in brand name clothes. There are dickwads in all walks of life. It doesn't take a degree to punch a woman—or try to kill her— but there are plenty of doctors and lawyers and executives that beat on their women. We had one just recently, a blood specialist for chrissakes, that beat his wife unconscious, then wrapped her in a rug—a Persian rug for chrissake—and dumped her in the bush, out beyond the city limits. Tried to bury her, but I guess the peckerhead wasn't used to manual labour. He gave up, and just left her there like she was a piece of garbage he didn't need. He obviously thought she was dead. Some doctor. She wasn't. She found us. She's not doing so good, but she's better than dead. That's the kicker. These guys have power. How do you go to a doctor for help, if your husband's that doctor's boss? How do you go to the cops, if your guy's a cop, too? It's sick.

It's like there's no way out for these women."

CALLER B: "My sister, she's married to a cop, and the stuff he does to her, it just makes me crazy. But she won't leave. What can you do with that? She won't leave. She just says he's gonna get her no matter what she does. It's like she's given up hope."

CALLER C: "Okay, okay, that's enough beating on cops, already. You think we're all animals? You think we don't have scruples? Yeah, sure, there are some of those cops you hear about, the ones you see in the movies that cheat the system, that got no rules, that make their own laws. Sure there are some. But they're not everybody. It's hard to work with those guys, and they taint the uniform, man, they make it all a sham. But some of us, we're just trying to do good. We're just trying to . . . Jesus . . . we're just trying to keep people safe . . ."

The caller's voice cracks, breaks off.

STAN: "I feel your pain, man."

CALLER C: "You don't know. You don't know what it's like to see the shit people get into, man. The way they threaten . . . everything. You'd have bars on all your windows if you knew what went on out there, man. It's ugly. So god damn ugly. And all you can do is follow the law. You want to beat the living shit out of some of the scum out there, but you can't. You know? You just can't become what they are. You know? You just wanta . . . you wanta be a MAN. You wanta

STAND for something. You want it all to MEAN something when you're done, by the time you die. And it just never stops. You just see ugly all the time and it gets that you can't tell the difference, you can't tell when something's right or when it's wrong. It gets all mixed up."

STAN: "All you can do is your best, man. That's it."

CALLER C: "We have a code, you know? A code that says that we can't abuse our position, can't use it to gain favours or manipulate people. We swear, when we become cops, to uphold the law and do it selflessly. Every day. Every night. In all situations. To take responsibility. Do you know how hard it is to walk up to some guy in a SUIT, and tell him that he's under arrest? To walk right into his workplace, and slap the cuffs on him in front of EVERYBODY? You can tear a guy down in seconds, and you gotta do it believing that you're RIGHT. Jesus. Who the hell knows all the time that they're RIGHT?"

STAN: "The phone lines are goin' crazy, now. Who's up next?"

PHONE LINE ONE: "It's Martin. I'm a big wheeler."

STAN: "A truck driver."

PHONE LINE ONE: "Yeah. I want to say a bit about being a dad, about being a man. I work hard. I'm on the road longer than most people are awake. It's my job to be gone. What's a guy to do when he's gotta be gone? I got two kids. I love those kids like I love my own body. Like they're ME. But I can't be there for them. I gotta be on the road. What can I do about that? Does that make me a neglecting dad? Do I have to worry now about my kids going blind 'cause I can't be there for them? Shit!"

STAN: "Anybody got something to say to that?"

PHONE LINE TWO: "Hell. You can't blame yourself for everything. I'm not employed. I got downsized fourteen months ago. Any severance I got is gone. Severance: does that mean I was fired? I don't even know. They call these things 'exit packages', but what does that mean? They buy you off. They wash their hands of you. Can't find work now. I'm in my fifties. My daughter wants to get married. Twenty thousand dollars she says is the average cost of a wedding. AVERAGE. Hell. It makes me shake just to think about it. You coddle these kids and give them everything, and they think the money grows on trees. They think it will never stop. Hell. I did, too. And now I can't get a job to save my life. That hurts."

PHONE LINE THREE: "That last caller, you gotta keep looking. You can't give up. I got three kids, all grown, and two of them still live at home. In their thirties. Nobody's hiring they say. Maybe. But I don't know. They don't know how to work these days. They stay up all night playing video games. In their thirties! And me, I should be retiring, but I can't. First of all, I don't want to come home to a houseful of kids. I wanted that to be over now. Somebody's got to show these kids how to live. And I . . . I hate to admit it, but I just don't know how."

PHONE LINE FOUR: "Crap. All crap. If that was my kid, I'd beat the shit out of him. My wife, she's got this son. He's nineteen, and useless as the day he was born. I can't stand the sight of him. He's got attitude like you've never seen. Acting like he's the man of the house or something. Crap! He's NOTHING! You gotta show these kids. It's all about respect. And respect and fear are the same damn . . ."

The sound of emergency sirens cuts the caller off.

STAN: "Sorry, man, but you are GONE. Next caller. Let's clear that last stink out of the air. Hello?"

WOMAN CALLER: "Hello? This is Amanda."

STAN: "Go ahead, Amanda."

WOMAN CALLER: "I'm part of a blended family. Your last caller, he's a woman's worst nightmare. You get out of one bad marriage, and when you move into the next one, you wonder. What's this guy like? Are my kids going to like him? Are we going to be able to make a family? My husband's got three kids from his first marriage, and I have three. I can tell you, we're no Brady Bunch. Makes me wonder about

Timothy, that little boy who calls in. Maybe he's better off in his original family. With his own dad. Even if the dad isn't perfect. Even if he's bad, maybe. I don't know. Maybe father knows best."

MAN CALLER 1: "No. No. Not every father knows best. I . . . I . . . You get your kid to sign up for the forces, just to get him out of the basement. To teach the kid some responsibility, some sense of purpose, right? To make a man out of him. And he takes a plane to a foreign country . . . and he dies there. Blown to bits. All busted up. You don't even think the war is real, it's just . . . politics. But your kid doesn't come back. He's just gone. It's real. Those wars far from home, they ask for our support and we give it. We give it in our taxes and at the Walmart checkout counter and on bumper stickers, and we send the best thing we got to give: our kids. And who's supporting THEM? Those beautiful, grown up Timothys? They're just dying, is all. They're just dead. There's no reason to it. None at all."

WOMAN CALLER 2 *(her voice trembles with age)*: "My husband—he's dead now—but he was in the war. He served his country, or someone's country. He came back. He was fine. All of him. No parts missing. No drinking problem. Just fine. But in his head, he was empty. Bored, I think. I think he used up all his valour, all his honour, out there, wherever he was. He came back all used up, and he just spent the rest of his life wandering around aimlessly. Bored, really. Shell shock maybe, who knows."

STAN: "Too much trauma. He'd seen too much."

WOMAN CALLER 2: "Maybe. How can you tell what goes on in someone's head? All I know is that he never settled down again, he never stopped staring off into space, looking for something to believe in. Now that he's gone, and it's all over—our family, our marriage—I wonder if he just would have been better off dying there. In his glory. Better off dead than alive."

STAN: "Hmm. Thanks for that. A different angle on things, isn't it, with Remembrance Day just around the corner. I've never thought before about how differently you might view life if you had to go to war. I'd always thought it would be hell. But I can see now that it might give you a sense of purpose. A sense of justice."

Stan pats the red poppy on his jacket lapel.

STAN: "Crazy world. Let's take another caller. We're on a roll tonight."

MAN CALLER 2: "Yo. Stan. Don't kid yourself. There's a war out there. Brian here. I'm a taxi driver. Well, I was. I'm on leave at the moment. Post-traumatic stress, they call it. Whatever you call it, it's bad. Can't sleep. Can't eat much. That's why I'm up."

The man on the phone exhales, as if he's smoking a cigarette.

STAN: "Tell us what happened to you, Brian."

MAN CALLER 2: "I was . . . I was in this accident. Sort of. Or I witnessed it. Both, I guess. This . . . this shooter, he tore up a mall. It was some kind of gang thing, they said. He came out when I was doing a drop off. He . . . he shot up my car. He killed the woman in the back seat. She was just going shopping. She . . . she wasn't doing anything wrong, she was just going shopping. I got so . . . ungh . . . I pushed on the gas, instead of the brake. I flattened the gun man against the wall. I got a hero badge. The mayor . . . the paper . . . but it was just a fluke. His gun went off like fireworks. I thought I was going to die. I thought I was going to die."

STAN: "Man. Oah. Wow. Man. I'm sorry, Brian. Wow. Whoo. Time for a little break, boys and girls and everyone in between and beyond. Here's a little comfort for Brian, for all of us, from Eric Clapton and his guitar."

Stan lets the first few bars ring through the studio: "Would you call my name, if I saw you in heaven?" STAN'S MAMA appears, alone, looking away from Stan. She is dressed in a black, long sleeved dress, with a veiled hat on her head. Her fat little hands clutch a small black plastic purse, from which she takes a white tissue. Her shoulders are shaking.

Stan rises and goes to her without thinking.

STAN: "Mom. Why are you crying, Mama? You hated him. You LEFT him." *Stan draws out the word like an accusation. She won't look at him.*

STAN'S MAMA: "It wasn't s'pposed to be like this. It wasn't."

STAN: "You took him away from me, Mom. You stole him. You made him leave."

STAN'S MAMA shakes her head.

STAN'S MAMA: "He had to leave, Stan. He HAD to. But I never made him do the things he did. I never took anything away from you, my happy boy. He did that all on his own. And he did it to both of us."

Stan's arms are like weights at his side. He watches his mother walk away, never looking back.

MAN ON LINE 1: "Are we on again? Stan? Hello?"

STAN: "You're live in three, two, one. . ."

MAN ON LINE 1: "Hi. I'm a local Union negotiator. I can tell you what's wrong with all of this: our society, our workplace. Our lives. It's politics. It's all politics. The greed head capitalists are making a mockery of human lives. There's no dignity in being human anymore. All your hard work is going into the pockets of a handful of money hungry corporations. Did you know that corporations actually lobby to have protection for their corporate properties over human life? So that, if there's a fire, for instance, that the firefighters have to save the property first, and the people last? Insanity. And that's who's running our governments, our businesses, and our world."

WOMAN ON LINE 2: "Here's a twist for you. I'm a CEO. A chief executive officer. One of those creeps at the top who keep getting bonuses even as their companies go under. That's me. I'm one of those. I've worked hard for what I've . . ."

STAN: "We all work hard, lady."

WOMAN ON LINE 2: "Alright. I concede. But . . . maybe all the hype is true. I never thought I'd see the day when I'd be siding with a union rep, but today . . . I found out something. Something I never thought possible. My company has an insurance policy on my head."

STAN: "Just on your head?"

WOMAN ON LINE 2: "Ha. No. On my life."

STAN: "Well, that makes sense, doesn't it? You're a big executive, your productivity is essential to the company, if you're lost then the company flounders. They need you. Right?"

WOMAN ON LINE 2: "That's what I thought at first. I was even flattered. But then I looked into it a little more. There are a bunch of us, hand selected it seems, that the company carries life policies on. At all levels. Mostly healthy, youngish people. So the premiums probably aren't high. But the amounts of coverage are. What that tells me is that my company sees me as an investment. An insurance crap shoot. They're HOPING I die. Then they collect. And the insurance they collect is worth more to the company—is a better investment— than all the work I do for them. I'm here at what? Four-thirty in the morning, already working, and I'd be of more use to my company if I did absolutely nothing except DIE. Makes me livid."

Stan whistles.

STAN: "Makes you wonder why we try so hard, doesn't it."

Stan pauses, contemplating the landscape of reflective wall before him.

STAN: "Oh! That reminds me! I've got a special message for y'all from Fenckels Ford, the thinking man's dealership."

Stan cues the ad, with its familiar trumpet blast, then mutes it. He sits back against the backrest of his chair, his ample head in the nest of his hands, eyes closed. His beefy arms extend like wings behind his head.

The phone rings. Stan pokes at the handset, and Timothy's voice comes on the line.

TIMOTHY: "Hullo, mister Temple. It's me, Timothy. I couldn't get my mom's phone easy tonight. She brought her purse into her room and I had to wait a long time until she and my dad stopped yelling and then fell asleep before I could sneak in and get it. And my dad's sleeping on the couch downstairs, so I have to be especially quiet."

STAN: "That's okay, Timothy. I'm glad you called."

Stan inserts a flourish of cello and piano

into the cue.

STAN: "Good evening, good morning, all you wandering souls out on this cold, stormy night. This is Stan, the Temple Man, still awake and still searching the skies for signs of sanity. We have Timothy on the line, tonight. How are you tonight, Timothy?"

TIMOTHY: "Good."

STAN: "That's good to hear. What's on your mind these days?"

TIMOTHY: "I'm wondering why my dad is sleeping on the couch."

STAN: "Mmhmm. One of life's mysteries, for certain. What else are you thinking, son?"

Stan steals a swig from his little flask, jiggles it around, eyeballing it. Watches the light play along its edges. Puts it down on the table, where the light can hit it. Rubs his hands before it as if it is a small, silver campfire.

TIMOTHY: "The wind is kinda scary outside. There's banging on my window. I don't like it."

Stan nods.

STAN: "Trees outside your window. I used to have that when I was a kid."

TIMOTHY: "Sounds like someone trying to get in."

STAN: "It's that kind of night, isn't it, Timothy? Spooky."

TIMOTHY: "Yeah."

STAN: "Are you afraid of the dark,

Timothy?"

A long pause.

TIMOTHY: "Wull. I have the light on now."

STAN: "Mmm. So the light doesn't scare you?"

Stan looks around the darkened studio. He takes another swig. Then another. The darkness seems to encroach, to deepen. He takes another swig. Replaces the flask under its spotlight.

TIMOTHY: "Nah. I feel better when its day. No one steals people during the day."

STAN: "Well, actually . . . huh! That's true, that's true, no doubt. Nothing bad happens in the light."

Stan watches as his dad appears out of the shadows, and stands with a suitcase before the open studio door. Stan's dad looks out the door for a long moment, then looks toward the floor over his shoulder, away from Stan. And he leaves, disappearing into the white light of the hallway beyond the studio.

TIMOTHY: "What about you, mister Temple? You afraid of the dark?"

Stan shakes his head, takes another swig. Shakes the flask, which is empty now. He deposits the metal container in his breast pocket and pats it.

STAN: "No, not big Stan the Temple Man. Nothing scares me. I've got a heart made of lead. Like the Tin Man in the Wizard of Oz."

TIMOTHY: "I don't know that story."

Stan nods, smiles.

STAN: "So, fine listeners out there, how can we respond to Timothy tonight?"

CALLER ONE: "Hi Timothy. Maybe your dad's just got a headache. Maybe that's why he's on the couch. Or a hangover."

CALLER TWO: "Maybe your dad's just lost, Timothy. Grown-ups have big troubles sometimes, and they can feel scared, too. I'm a junky, and I felt bad all the time, until I gave it up. I found God, and that helped me give up drugs and start living."

Stan takes the flask out of his pocket, to look at it. He looks back through the open door, where his father disappeared only minutes ago.

CALLER TWO: "There's a program called twelve steps. But the first step is the hardest. You have to admit that you are powerless against your addiction, and that you need help from someone bigger than you. You need to listen hard for God's voice, and give yourself over to Him."

TIMOTHY: "My mom says mister Temple sounds like God. 'Cause he has such a big voice. It makes me wonder sometimes if God would use the Internet and the phone to talk to you. You know, straight on. That would be good."

CALLER TWO: "That sounds mighty fine, Timothy. It does. I wish it were that simple."

Stan looks at the flask in his hand, uncaps it, turns it upside down. He sets it on the work station table, on its neck, and places the cap beside it.

Then he laughs, a big, booming laugh, which he has to force to come out.

STAN: "Maybe it is that simple, Timothy. If I were really God, what would I say to you?"

TIMOTHY: "I dunno."

STAN: "There must be something you're wishing to hear. You keep calling."

TIMOTHY: "Yeah. Wull, I guess I'd like to know how to sleep again. I don't feel so good much anymore."

CALLER THREE: "Hi there. Mister Templeman, this is Angela. I hate to be argumentative, but, what Timothy needs is not God. It's a good mother. I tried for nearly twelve years to have a baby. Invitro treatments finally worked after the third time. And then there were five babies. It was the hardest thing in the world to pick which babies should survive."

TIMOTHY: "You didn't keep them all?"

CALLER THREE: "I couldn't keep them all, Timothy. Five babies! I'm forty-three years old. I kept two. My two perfect babies."

Newborn cries interrupt, and continue through the call, getting louder.

CALLER THREE: "There is nothing in this world I wouldn't give up for my two babies. I would die for them. Your mother should remember how she would die for you."

STAN: "Okey dokey. Let's move on to the

next caller, shall we?"

CALLER FOUR: "Speaking of sleep deprivation, I'm a student, and here it is almost five in the morning and I still haven't done my homework for this week. My profs are going to kill me, and I'm getting that I just don't care. What they are asking us to do is impossible! Some of them are downright bullies. So I'm doing all this work, and for what? There are no jobs out there. I need all this education to get exactly nowhere. It makes no sense."

CALLER FIVE: "Howdy. This is Tara. I just had to call in about hard work. Okay. I'm a housewife, alright? Yeah. I've got this houseful of kids and dogs and goldfish, and all I do is work. I get no paycheck. I get no thanks. I get no retirement plan. It's all just sweat."

STAN: "So why do it, Tara? What do you gain?"

Caller Five stammers.

CALLER FIVE: "Um, I get to sleep in, sometimes. I get to take a day off when I want to. I get to see my kids in their school plays, and help on hot dog day. There are perks."

CALLER SIX: "Perks! Shit! I've got to live on energy drinks to keep going! I'm a security guard on the night shift, AND I got three kids at home. All the stuff that Tara has to do I have to do too! Without the sleeping in! Some people just got no gratitude for what they get."

CALLER SEVEN: "This is Erica. I'm up so

late because the pain is too bad, I just can't sleep. I wish all these women would just stop complaining. They've got homes and husbands and kids, and I got nothing but a puffy face and sore boobs."

STAN: "Erica?"

CALLER SEVEN: "I got out of surgery yesterday, but the swelling just isn't going down."

STAN: "You had cosmetic surgery. Aah. How old are you, Erica?"

CALLER SEVEN: "Twenty-nine. And I'm not getting any younger."

Stan snickers and hangs his head.

CALLER SEVEN: "Go ahead and laugh, but have you tried being a woman lately? Plastic is the only answer."

The caller clicks off.

STAN (not unkindly): "Erica, my darling, I hope your Tylenol threes kick in soon. I feel for you, girl, I do. Who am I to judge? I'm just a big, lonely guy."

He looks at the upside down flask.

STAN: "With a drinking problem. We all have our dark days, people. We are all in this together."

TIMOTHY: "Mister Temple? You're just kidding about those 'dark days', right? The darkness is a night thing, right? I don't think I could handle more darkness all the time."

Timothy's voice blurs.

STAN: "Timothy. Tim. Move your face away from the phone, son. Thanks."

TIMOTHY: "Sorry."

LINE 1: "This is Father Jerry. What are we all rushing to keep up with? God means taking time. . ."

LINE 2: "Church is full of shit, top to toe."

LINE 3: "Gotta believe in something. My wife suffers from depression. Despair kills. We're not built to be alone."

LINE 4: "But we are alone. We isolate ourselves: social media, online porn, this phone talk show, even? We're all sitting alone, miles apart, talking to strangers instead of our families and friends."

LINE 5: "Even Timothy: he's talking to us, a bunch of empty voices, instead of talking to his mom and his dad, like he should. Telling THEM he's scared, or he's mad . . ."

STAN: "Are you mad, Timothy? Mad at your dad? Is that why you wish he'd go live somewhere else?"

Timothy sighs.

TIMOTHY: "Wull, he never comes to any of my soccer games. He makes me treat him with respect, but he doesn't do that for me. He's gone all the time. He swears at me, and stops me from doing things, and he makes all these rules. And he snaps at me anytime I do even the littlest thing wrong. It's not fair."

LADY ON ONE: "The lad's right, that's

not fair."

MAN ON TWO: "Double standard."

WOMAN ON THREE: "Someone ought to call in the. . ."

MALE VOICE ON TIMOTHY'S LINE: "Hello? Hello? Is someone on the line? Timothy, what on earth are you doing up at this . . ."

Timothy's line clicks off.

STAN: "Oh oh."

WOMAN ON THREE: "Lord forgive us! What have we done!"

ACT II, Scene 2
Grace

The studio door opens. Stan fills the doorway, looking ragged and weary. He slumps against the doorframe, reaches for a sliding light switch on the studio wall, and flicks it up to the top level with his index finger. Brilliant light tears into the room, buzzing aggressively. Stan groans and covers his eyes.

The studio is dingier than expected. There are food wrappers and dried puddle marks on the floor and table. Stan approaches the bank of windows separating his studio space from the engineer's room beyond, and squints at his own reflection. He sticks out his tongue. Rubs his face. Assesses his girth.

Then he makes his way, slowly, to his desk

chair. He begins to remove his coat, but then shivers, and elects to keep it on, smoothing the lapel with the bright red poppy. Looks at the clock. It is one minute to midnight.

He groans heavily and stations himself at the mike. With one fat finger he cues the flourish of sound that precedes his show, wincing deeply at the noise.

STAN: "Goood midnight, lovers and lazies out there. This is Stan, your not-so Temple Man, on the line and er-raring to go."

Stan rubs his face and smacks his lips together, looking for drink. The upside down flask still stands in the middle of the work station table, useless and empty. In the harsh fluorescent overhead lighting, the metal tin looks dull, lifeless.

STAN: "The night is young, and the future bright. So call me, people; keep me up at night."

Stan chuckles, deep in his belly.

STAN: "The lines are as open as my ears, my flock. Call in, and share your worries with your world."

The lines fire up.

STAN: "You're on, line one."

WOMAN ON LINE ONE: "Hi Stan. This is Diane."

STAN: "Hi Diane."

WOMAN ON LINE ONE: "I heard your show last night, Stan. You said something about a drinking problem."

STAN: "Uh huh. That's the first step, isn't

it?"

WOMAN ON LINE ONE: "I think so. I'm not that sure. See, I'm calling about another addiction. An addiction to food. I'm morbidly obese, and I've struggled forever in my relationship with food."

STAN: "There's your problem right there, Diane. You have a RELATIONSHIP with food. Maybe what you need is to have more one night stands."

WOMAN ON LINE ONE: "Very funny ha ha."

MAN ON LINE TWO: "She's got a point, Stan. Food can be tricky. My sister's anorexic. She doesn't eat at all, and what she does eat has to be eaten by all these rules. Only so many wedges of orange. Only so many bites of sandwich, chewed a specific number of times."

STAN: "How's she making out?"

MAN ON LINE TWO: "Not good. She's dying of kidney failure. Or liver. One of those important organs. She's starved herself to death. Breaks my heart."

LADY ON LINE THREE: "Hi Stan. All night pharmacy here. I heard the conversation about food, and eating disorders. There's a new disorder on the books: ortho-rexia. It's when you get so obsessed with eating the RIGHT foods that you make yourself nuts. It's a dangerous and as bad for your health as the self-starvation of anorexia."

STAN: "Sheesh. Won't our own minds ever leave us alone? Next caller: can you save the day?"

CALLER A: "This is Sharongit from Weight Watchahs. I've been listening to the comments and I have some sug-jestions for your listenahs. Some of the foods you eat are actually bettah for you than you think. For instance, ketchup is considered by Weight Watchahs to be a vedgetable."

Stan freezes for a moment, then leans forward, eyeball to eyeball with the mike.

STAN: "Ketchup . . . is a vegetable."

CALLER A: "Yes, that's correct. And so is popcorn. A full cup of air-popped popcorn is equivalent to a half cup serving of corn. It's just as good for you as a vedgetable. It IS a vedgetable."

CALLER B: "So I suppose relish is a vegetable, too. Made of cucumbers, right?"

CALLER A: "That's correct. So you see, eating well is not so very difficult, in the end. It's all about portion control."

STAN: "What do you think about that, Diane? Does the knowledge that ketchup is a vegetable ease your burden at all?"

WOMAN ON LINE ONE: "Well . . . it does, actually. It does."

Stan chuckles heartily. He squints at his girth rumbling clearly in the mirror walls of the sound studio.

STAN: "It makes me feel better, too. Bring on the junk food."

CALLER A: "That's not egg-zactly what I said, Stan, I just meant that Weight Watchahs . . ."

STAN: "You made your point quite brilliantly, Sharongit, you really did. We'll be back in a moment to explore more of life's little secrets, after this word from our sponsors. . ."

Stan allows a digital ad to play, followed by a short musical blip to fill the time while he searches the studio for something to drink.

He rummages under his coat, through his bag, around the pedestal foot of the work station table. Finally, he finds a can, rattles it, and hears the sound of liquid.

He pours the fluid down his gullet, winces a bit, then grins.

STAN: "Flat," *he says,* "but wet." *With a flick he's back on air.* "Alright, Alright, the night is warming up. You're with Stan, the increasingly Temple-like Man, bopping through this November eve with miracles on our minds. So far tonight, we've solved the dietary problems of Diane, a self-confessed woman of size. Junk food—or at least condiments—are NOT out. Anything is possible. We're looking for more words of wisdom. Line six, who's on the line?"

TIMOTHY: "It's me, mister Temple."

Stan gasps audibly, and runs to the mike, smiling at it as though it were the embodiment of Timothy's face.

STAN: "Timothy! It's you!"

TIMOTHY: "Yup." *The child yawns loudly.* "But I can only talk for a minute. I had to go pee."

STAN: "So you're sleeping."

TIMOTHY: "Yeah. Last night, when dad caught me on the phone with you . . . well, I tol' him how scared I was about somebuddy sneakin' in my room. He apologized for scaring me. He said he just got scared himself, 'caus'o' somethin' that happened on the bus he drives, a while ago."

STAN: "Your dad's a bus driver. That's why he's gone so much."

TIMOTHY: "Mmhmm. He said he doesn't sleep so good now, after what happened. He didn't tell me what it was, but it must 'ave ben bad. So he stayed in my room last night. He even opened the window."

STAN: "Didn't you get cold?"

TIMOTHY: "Nope. Dad slept right in my bed. Boy! Does he get hot at night! He's not there now, though. He's still up with my mom. I can hear them down in the living room."

STAN: "What are they doing?"

Timothy listens, and Stan listens along with him.

TIMOTHY: "They're laughing."

Stan's eyebrows lift.

STAN: "That's good news, Timothy."

TIMOTHY: "Yeah. Oh. And you can call me Tim."

Stan balks at the microphone.

STAN: "Really! How did you pull THAT off!?"

TIMOTHY: "Wull, I tol' dad that I liked Tim better. He said okay. He just wanted to call me Timothy, 'cause he thought Tim sounded too much like a bus driver's name."

Stan looks at his mike, and laughs. The sound grows bigger, softening the harsh light in the studio, warming up the space.

STAN: "Well, good for you, Tim. Good for you."

TIMOTHY: "Yup. Goodnight, mister Temple. Thanks for all the talking."

And the line clicks off.

Stan looks around the room, at its grimy reality. He looks at the expanse of mirrored windows reflecting his every movement. He looks at the upside-down flask, and rights it. He takes the red poppy from his coat lapel, and positions it in the flask, where it pivots happily for a second, then settles.

Stan grabs the mike again, and reaches for the sliding wall switch. He urges the switch lower, and the lighting in the studio dims a little. Stan breathes in, and out, and his shoulders relax.

STAN: "It is time to turn it *dowwwn,* all you lusty, rusty souls and sisters in our sleeping city. Let's get cozy. Call in. Share your secrets, and your solutions. You're with Stan, the Temple Man, and you're among friends."

THE END

ABOUT THE AUTHOR

Jennifer Rouse Barbeau is a trade-published author, professional illustrator, and full-time college professor. She is both author and illustrator of the novel *Swampy Jo* (Your Scrivener Press), and illustrator of the children's book *La Laineuse* by Rachel Desaulniers (Centre FORA), and the non-fiction fact book *Come On Over! Northeastern Ontario A to Z* by Dieter Buse and Graeme Mount (Your Scrivener Press). Her writing has appeared in Canadian national magazines as well as in the anthology *Bluffs: Northeastern Ontario Stories from the Edge* (Your Scrivener Press) and *Sulphur: Laurentian University's Literary Journal* (Laurentian Printing). She lives and works in northern Ontario, Canada, with husband and author Barry Grills.